For Lex, Ginger, Bonny and everlasting George.

Published in 2017 by Melbournestyle Books

Melbournestyle Books
155 Clarendon Street, South Melbourne
Victoria 3205, Australia
www.melbournestyle.com.au

National Library of Australia
Cataloguing-in-Publication entry:

Coote, Maree, author, illustrator.

Title: Robyn Boid: architect / Maree Coote

ISBN: 9780992491741 (hardback)

1. Architects—Juvenile fiction
I. Coote, Maree, ill. II.Title

Dewey Number: A823.4

Design by Maree Coote
Printed in China

10 9 8 7 6 5 4 3 2

ROBYN BOID: ARCHITECT

Written and illustrated by Maree Coote

Robyn Boid lived at the National University,
high up on a ledge of the Architecture School.

Her nest overlooked a skyline of spectacular shapes,
and each day, while she studied domes and spires and minarets,
she listened to the class through the window.

When I grow up, I'd like to be an architect, thought Robyn.

As she listened, she learned there was much more
to architecture than building. There were complex ideas like:
'Are round nests always best?' and *'Think outside the circle.'*
And the biggest question of all:
'What comes first: the nest, or the egg?'

It turned her thinking upside-down.

Robyn was the first Boid to go to university, and she wanted to do well. So she set to work practising all the important shapes like circles, squares, triangles, rectangles, and domes.

I can think outside the circle, thought Robyn,
and she turned her own nest upside-down.
It's a dome! she discovered,
and she added another small dome on top.
It was as good as any on the skyline.
But where does my egg fit in? she wondered.

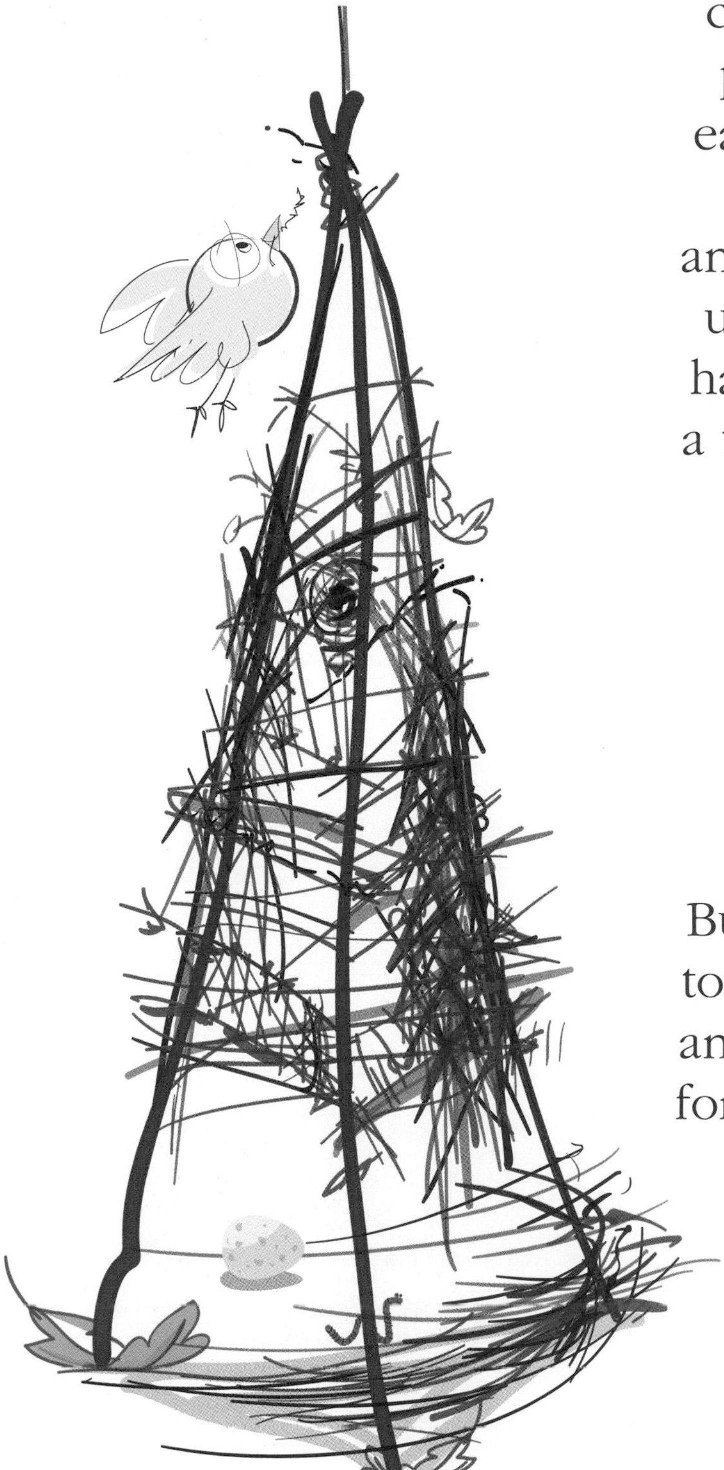

Next,
she tried
a tall,
thin
triangle,
carefully
placing
each twig
higher
and higher
until she
had made
a towering
spire.

But was it
too pointy
an address
for an egg?

Robyn coiled circles into cylinders and cones,
stretched squares into rectangles and cubes,
and tilted triangles up into pyramids.

Before long
she was making
towers with turrets,
and battlements
with parapets...

But was it all
too grand
for an egg?

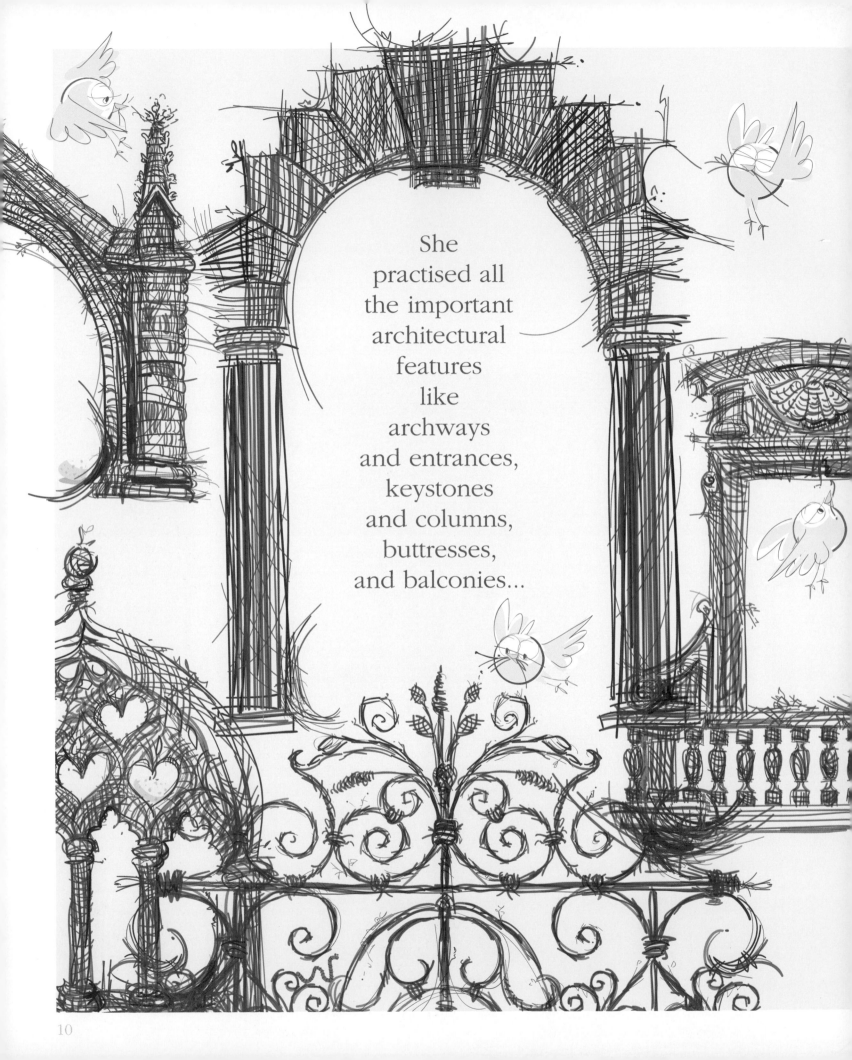

She
practised all
the important
architectural
features
like
archways
and entrances,
keystones
and columns,
buttresses,
and balconies...

She built
capitals
with
curlicues;
bridges
with
balustrades;
pedestals,
patterns
and
plinths.

She soon
learned
that a nest is
not a nest...

...if there's
nowhere
for an egg
to rest.

Robyn flew over the university, and far beyond.
The more she built, the more she learned
about shape and space, symmetry and scale.

She practised pagodas
and perfected pavilions...

...but was this the
best nest for an egg?

She did
home work
and field work
and some
pretty fancy
stick work...

She
worked
on her
towers
for
hours
and
hours...

She mixed
textures
and
colours...

...tried
stacking,
cantilever
and tilt...

(but found
towers
quite windy
once built.)

Robyn spiralled all the way up on the inside...

...and
spiralled
all the
way
down
on the
outside.

But
was this
the right
shape
for her
nest?

She soon realised that there were endless possibilities
for shape and design.

So what was the *best* shaped nest for an egg?

And then, out of the blue, the idea came to her:
Egg-xactly the right shape for an egg is...

Elevation

Plan
Scale: 1:1

Fig. 4

...egg-shaped.

Suddenly, her work became truly egg-xciting!
She designed egg-xtraordinary apartments
and egg-xceptional homes.
And now she understood three very important things:

1. A bird can live anywhere, but an egg needs a nest.
2. Thinking outside the circle can lead to egg-xcellent ideas.
3. The egg comes first.

By the end
of her studies,
Robyn had become
an egg-xpert builder and
an egg-xceptional
designer...

...famous for outdoor places and indoor spaces full of sunshine, breezes, shelter and shade.

Architecture is like an egg,
thought Robyn,
...full of egg-xciting possibilities.

Which gave her the idea
for a book on her career.
Perhaps she'd call it:
'Great Egg-xpectations'
by Robyn Boid: Architect.

HIDE & FIND FUN

CAN YOU COUNT 34 speckled eggs in this book?

Robyn Boid's favourite breakfast is a nice fat worm.
CAN YOU FIND 14 wiggly worms hidden in this book?

CLEVER KIDS TEACHERS' NOTES:

Discover architecture with ROBYN BOID's favourite words:

ARCHWAY: a curved symmetrical structure spanning the upper part of an entrance.

ASYMMETRY: when one side of a thing is not the mirror image of the other side.

BATTLEMENT: a low wall on top of a castle with square openings for shooting through.

BALCONY: a platform outside an upstairs window.

BALUSTRADE: a railing fence on a balcony or bridge.

BUTTRESS: a support structure of stone or brick, built against a wall to strengthen and hold the wall upright.

CANTILEVER: a long beam fixed at only one end, projecting out beyond its vertical support, and held in place by fixture or weight at the support end only.

CAPITAL: the top section of a column – sometimes quite simple and sometimes highly decorative.

CURLICUE: an intricate ornamental curl or twist.

COLUMN: an upright pillar, usually cylindrical.

DOME: a half-sphere shaped roof.

EAVES: the overhanging edges of a roof.

KEYSTONE: the top central stone of an archway which locks neighbouring stones into place by exerting pressure down both sides of the arch.

MINARET: a tall, slender tower with a balcony.

PAVILION: a light, ornamental building, normally for recreation.

PLINTH: a block of stone or wood used as a base for a pillar or statue.

PEDESTAL: a base for a statue or column.

PAGODA: a tiered tower with multiple eaves.

PARAPET: a defensive wall around the top of a building

TURRET: a small tower on top of a larger tower or at the corner of a castle wall.

TILT: placing things at an angle – not horizontal or vertical.

TOWER: a tall narrow building, sometimes part of a church or castle.

SPIRE: the tall, tapering roof of a tower.

SYMMETRY: when opposite halves of a thing are the mirror image of each other.

SCALE: the size of things compared to their surroundings.

CLEVER KIDS TEACHERS' NOTES available online at
www.cleverkids.net.au

ROBYN BOID'S NEST-BUILDING WAS INSPIRED BY:

Sydney Opera House, Sydney, 1973 (Jørn Utzon) p.12

Wangu Pavilion, Lijiang, c1382 p.12

Saint Basil's Cathedral, Moscow, 1561 (Postnik & Barma Yakovlev)
and Bogolubskaya Church, Pushkino City, 1906, p.13

The Chrysler Building, New York, 1930 (William Van Alen) p.14

The Sydney Tower, Sydney, 1970 (Donald Crone) p.14

Eiffel Tower, Paris, 1889 (Gustave Eiffel) p.14

The Eureka Tower, Melbourne, 2006 (Fender Katsalidis Architects) p.14

Tower Reusel, The Netherlands, 2009 (Ateliereen Architecten) p.14

Sir Duncan Rice Library, University of Aberdeen, Scotland, 2012
(Schmidt Hammer Lassen Architects) p.16

Messner Mountain Museum, Corones, 2015 (Zaha Hadid Architects) p.18

Casa Lloyd, Melbourne, 1960 (Robin Boyd Architects) p.22 & 23

ACKNOWLEDGEMENTS & THANKS to: Ateliereen Architecten; Schmidt Hammer Lassen Architects;
Crone Architects; Fender Katsalidis Architects, and Zaha Hadid Architects.

SPECIAL THANKS to THE BOYD FOUNDATION for their kind advice and assistance.

**MELBOURNESTYLE
BOOKS**
www.melbournestyle.com.au